JOSHUA BALDWIN THE WILSHIRE SUN

TURTLE POINT PRESS

Lines from "Autobiography: Hollywood" by Charles
Reznikoff from *The Poems of Charles Reznikoff,
1918–1975*, edited by Seamus Cooney reprinted
by permission of Black Sparrow Books, an imprint
of David R. Godine, Publisher, Inc. Copyright
© 2005 by The Estate of Charles Reznikoff

FOR MY GRANDPARENTS

The cloudy afternoon is as pleasant
as silence. Who would think
one would ever have enough of sunshine?
A good epitaph, I suppose, would be
He liked the sunshine;
better still, *He liked to walk.*
And yet the dead, if it could speak, might say,
I had grown tired of walking,
yes, even of the sunshine.

CHARLES REZNIKOFF
"Autobiography: Hollywood"

I JUST LANDED IN LOS ANGELES. My older brother has been here two years, in the valley neighborhood of Encino. He makes his living as an importer of flowers, and resides comfortably alone in a one-story cube-shaped house. According to letters and phone conversations he feels "really wonderful."

I come as a writer, hoping to make a fortune in the movies. Hollywood is hiring these days. That's what Jerry told me. He's on his way here right now, some miles behind me (afraid of flying, he chose to take the train). "Come on," he persuaded me over beers three weeks ago, "we'll move out there and work together making easy money setting down screenplays both dumb and brilliant."

When I checked into my apartment building in Santa Monica the fellow at the desk handed me a postcard from Jerry.

Jacob—I'm laid over in a small Arizona town right now, thinking, over a glass of seltzer, why don't you like my novel? My opinion is that you're jealous of me. But I am also jealous of you and that complicates the matter.—Jerry

The letter startled me and sent a wave of nausea from my knees to my throat. I entered my room and set my white cap down on the wooden ironing board and stepped onto the little terrace for a cigarette, wondering, was I to consider this a threat from Jerry? And if so, how serious a threat? We met each other through our employ as assistants at a big Manhattan publishing firm. We both hated the day-in-day-out repetitive nonsense of the work, and our friendship, if you could call it that, consisted of complaining about the job in a coffee shop as we ate our egg salad and vinegar sandwiches and pulled viciously at glasses of coke during lunch hour.

I stubbed my cigarette out in an empty almond can, hurried down the dark stairwell of the apartment building and found a corner pay phone to call my brother and let him know that I'd arrived in Los Angeles.

To say the least, I am very excited to be in Los Angeles. Walking down Wilshire Boulevard towards the ocean, the bright sun calming my brain and setting all my spirits at ease, plus the light breeze blowing up my pants-legs; slipping inside the shady newspaper stores, the subdued but also jitterbug delicatessens; even passing the bums smirking into garbage cans and up at the gargantuan traffic lights—all of these things, though I can't say why, make me feel at home. I've never left the East before, and instead of any homesickness, I've several times gone so far as to speak aloud to myself today, and to the pigeons as well, "God almighty, this is the place."

Underneath my intense excitement, I feel an insane sadness, and this too, I love. Somehow, the sadness is filling me with joy. The utter loneliness of the blocks, the long—the endless!—blocks of houses extending north and south, and not a human being on either side except for a tiny faraway mother pushing a baby carriage up her front lawn, the sun hazily illuminating the infinity of the city. Drunk with health, I had to stop once and lean against some shuttered bank to stare across the street at an ancient green clock on the cornice of a building.

I felt real promise in the air this afternoon, and a rush at having disappeared from New York City and its gray, cold, close subway cars, its musty, dim, and crowded living rooms, and its harsh, moronic, tension-filled office-building routines of contracts, memorandums, errands, and telegrams.

I came upon a plaza of benches in front of an insurance firm headquarters and was struck with the impression that I'd landed in San Antonio, and scribbled some lousy jokes and bits of dialogue in my pad.

A bunch of palm trees were drooping over my head, filling me with a new desire—like for a new pair of shoes or a chocolate milkshake. I don't think I want to write scripts with Jerry; I would be better off writing, I think, a simple 200-page novel in my apartment. Listening to the buses swish by, rising early, the pages will definitely pour out of me with great ease.

The trick, of course, is to return to Los Angeles. Five days after my arrival I came down with a terrible fever, and my brother put me on the afternoon train to New York. "Los Angeles is no place for a young man with a fever," he said to me as he pushed me into my sleeper car. "Now, rest up—here, I'll close the curtains for you. Mother will meet you at Penn Station."

In my delirium I supposed my tongue was either missing or up in flames and I made no response to my brother, who appeared to be wearing an apron. Out of a front pouch he pulled a pack of cigarettes and a small jar of instant coffee granules. "For when you're feeling better, buddy boy," he said, patting me on my damp head. The last thing I remember of the Golden State is peeking at my brother through the curtains as he dissolved into a shimmering orange grove. I slept deep for three days, until the transfer in Chicago. Now I'm back in Brooklyn Heights, living with my mother and aunt, trying to figure my next move.

When my father killed himself five years ago, my aunt moved in. She helps my mother with the housework and generally tries to cheer her up with fashion magazines, card games, and conversation. Plus she keeps her away from the vodka. She allows her one vice: cigarettes. They smoke together on the stoop. They are sitting down there right now, and their chatter and smoke carries up to my room through the open window. I smoke too, and blow my smoke into their smoke.

I've been riding the buses around quite a lot, and going to movies, and eating hot dogs. I keep a large bag of peanuts under my desk. Shells cover the floor of my room. I think I will go to the Paramount building on Times Square tomorrow, for no particular reason. I will have to ride the subway—something I dread.

I took the subway to Grand Central Station, and before walking west to the Paramount building, I sat on a bench in the main waiting hall and drank a cup of watery lunch stand coffee. I stared at a telephone booth and considered calling my brother. I also thought about calling the apartment building in Santa Monica to ask the fellow at the desk if he happened to find a pen somewhere in my room.

It seems that I lost my pen in Los Angeles. Or maybe it fell out of my pocket on the train to New York. I don't know. I liked that pen, a fine Parker Jotter that my father brought back for me from England. He spent three months there about two years before he shot himself, on business—something to do with closing a linen deal with one of the major British retailers, Marks & Spencer I think. Well, I didn't make any phone calls, and then I looked down at my left tennis shoe and noticed a small tear at the point where the rubber toe meets the canvas, felt depressed, and walked to the Paramount building, where I stopped and looked up at the glittering script on the facade for a few seconds, and then proceeded to the subway and rode back to Brooklyn. I'm going to listen to baseball on the radio now, and try to fall asleep.

I had a dream last night that all different sizes of airplanes were buzzing around in the sky above the harbor. Most of the airplanes were simple silver, but one of them—a huge red and blue jetliner—carried a bunch of bullhorn wielding film directors on the wings. It seems they were directing a complicated scene on the Brooklyn Bridge. All of the cables on the bridge had been removed. I couldn't understand why there were multiple directors working on the one movie. Maybe some kind of competition was going on. Suddenly, I found myself seated in the cockpit of a rattling bomber, and the pilot told me that at the call of "Action!" I must jump out. He said it would be fine, that I would land in the water. Church bells up the street awoke me, and I went into the kitchen and sat at the table and drank a glass of iced tea.

My mother thinks I should call the publishing firm and ask for my position back. I told her that I'll be returning to Los Angeles the second week of June (in fact I haven't made any real arrangements) so there's really no point. She frowned, and my aunt, glaring at me, took her by the hand and said, "Let him go if he wants to, and besides his brother is there to look after him."

Then my mother, whimpering, asked me, "Jacob, why don't you just live with your brother if you really must go back to Los Angeles?"

I told her that if Jerry and I are to collaborate on scripts, we must be in the same neighborhood, and that the valley land is no place for screenwriters. Then my back started to hurt and I felt like screaming so I left the apartment and walked along Columbia Heights, by the water. Across the way, Manhattan was all lit up like a warehouse full of croaking soda vending machines, and the sight did nothing to assuage my impulse to scream—but still I didn't.

I am trying to determine where my laziness comes from. I've concluded that the source must be my grandfather, my mother's father, a gambling bum who lives in his deceased mother's apartment on Park Avenue.

I got out of bed this morning at 11:30. From 8:30 on I awoke every half-hour and told myself to get up, but then quickly answered myself with: "No, dreaming is good for writers—it's the same as writing, really," and rolled over. An idiotic idea, I recognized when I finally got up and had nothing to show for it, feeling gross and worthless.

But I've got to maintain a sense of dignity. So around 1

o'clock this afternoon I took a walk through my neighborhood and down to the piers, bringing along my little pad to take down some story notes. I wish I had an actress friend for whom I could write a script; that would give my project some push. The men up in Paramount would take a look straightaway if they knew the script was attached to one of the rising stars.

Then I recalled how I felt that day sitting under the palm trees in Santa Monica, filled with desire and cool confidence, and I got Chet Baker's rendition of "Look for the Silver Lining" in my head, and closed my eyes and tried to get to Los Angeles that way. But the moaning foghorns in the harbor prevented any prolonged reverie. I opened my eyes and saw the Staten Island Ferry crashing into the Manhattan slip, and I felt my body shift and knock in sympathy with the event. It's that game New York plays with natives, the city tells you that every idea you've got related to leaving is just a big trap you've set up for yourself, that there's nowhere else to go, and while you may be driven out in disgrace you can't just willfully depart.

I went to the bank today to check my balances and withdraw some petty cash. When my father died he left me a fair amount of money, just like he did for my mother and my brother, enough to give my own wife and children—should they ever exist—a fine lift. I didn't think I would touch the money for a long time; after all I'd been working enough to meet all of my modest expenses. Until I quit my job, that is, and went to Los Angeles at Jerry's urging. And now I'm not working on anything. All I am is a professional dodger, and until I'm back in Los Angeles I don't see myself making any kind of progress. Once there I'll start investing in myself, as the saying goes. Here in New York I'm of a mind to go over to my grandfather's and watch cartoons projected onto his dining room wall (and maybe the ceiling too) and take his pistol out of the bathroom cupboard and shoot at the pigeons congregating in the airshaft.

I went to a 3 o'clock showing of *Brass Rain* today. The movie opens with a close-up of a brown derby wrapped in blue cellophane, floating in a lagoon. Zooming out, we see the image is inside of a tabloid show on a television mounted high in the ceiling corner at a farmers' market dining patio. A young man wearing a white flannel suit sits on a metal chair, eating what looks like a fantastic whole-wheat and sugar dusted doughnut. He looks up at the television, and squinting at the derby, removes a pen from the inside pocket of his jacket and scrawls some illegible words on a piece of stationary from the Malibu California Surf Hotel. He waves his hand at a flea, a snare drum cracks, and the title sequence begins, a phantasmagoria of orange-saturated smashed soda bottles, burnt automobiles, and deserted barbershops.

When I got home I took a nap and dreamt that I was sitting by the movie's lagoon, photographing couples as they rowed around in circles eating tremendous hamburgers with blankets of American cheese drooping out from the bun. Then I was wandering around some French Quarter of Los Angeles, all of the bakers dumping flour off their balconies, and ended up behind the steaming Korean fast food stalls of Wilshire Boulevard. I hurried up when I realized I was on my way to my night job as a tile-scrubber at the Aztec Hotel.

Strolling around Coney Island today, I dropped a coin into a scale to learn my weight: 195 pounds. I looked at my reflection in the protective glass surrounding the bumper car court and was overcome with shame. I am a scruffy faced and plump good-for-nothing. But no! Lo! I'm just an Elvis Presley stunt-double in need of a shower, and I bought a cup of beer, sat down on a bench and watched the women wearing lightweight cardigan sweaters pass by, their breasts pointing out like great torpedoes of life. And I felt a little better, and I walked to the train station and riding home daydreamed about palm trees as I stared at the Statue of Liberty in the distance, from my outlook a mere teal phantom shrouded in smoke. I intend to buy a set of dumb-bells on Fulton Street tomorrow.

I awoke this morning extremely queasy and consumed with the feeling that I am the only person alive—at least on my block. I sat at my desk, lit a cigarette, flipped through my father's facsimile of the 1860 *Leaves of*

Grass—"afar on arctic ice, the she-walrus lying drowsily, / while her cubs play around;"—and dumped the bit of water remaining in my thermos onto my head. That would be my bath for the day. The cigarette tastes of wet cardboard, I announced to my naked feet. I must get moving, because I have been sitting in my room chewing my lip and turning my head from side to side quite a while now.

These past few days I have been occupied with a new project: writing letters to and from imaginary persons regarding Los Angeles. Some of the correspondents sound fairly insane, their voices echoing with the sort of bright-eyed lunacy that I think only Los Angeles allows, like:

> *To whom it may concern,*
> *And so I spoke, presumably, of laundry, and walked on.*
> *Probably on cause of being clean I proceeded to the bar*
> *and asked for my keys, then went up to my room to boil*
> *an egg. I'm off to Moab tomorrow for the weekend to re-*
> *trieve a case of vodka from Heck. You come to the party*
> *next Saturday at The Terrace in Brentwood, and bring*
> *a friend. It will be relaxing, I promise.*
> *Signed,*
> *F. F. Jones*

I wish I could have made it to the Central Library in downtown Los Angeles during my truncated stay in town. I went to the library by Prospect Park yesterday and looked at images of the place in a volume called *Book Civilization in Los Angeles*. I sunk into a pleasant daze for more than an hour, and intermittently recorded this exchange between friends:

> *Tom,*
>
> *I saw a great number of women crying today, inside the cars and delis. I notice the women are treated far more poorly here than in New York. I believe my girlfriend in Culver City is afraid of me, because that is a natural feeling towards a fellow here. This is a pretty barbaric place, seems to be dark and late even in the middle of the morning. When will you be coming out? I can set you up in the hills, perhaps; or, if you like, Topanga Canyon where it's quiet and you could get a screenplay done in a week I bet.*
>
> *Your pal,*
> *Zev*

Zev,

How nice it is nice of you to write, but I don't think you understand anything about me anymore, not at all. You're my friend so I imagine you can at least understand that. Here I am in a top-floor stuffy office in the garment district certainly planning my escape from this damned city (if I don't get out soon they'll have to give me a cane, and I'm only 32) to come out there to sit poolside and churn out scripts quick as I drink ice whiskey, ice whiskey, ice whiskey. But what with my wife out of work and the babies in need of new clothes I don't know if I can swing the travel expense. If you could lend me cash for the bus fare I assure you I'll pay you back. You know I'll reimburse you fast if you just put me up in Topanga like you say and shut the doors etc.

Take care,

Tom

It seems these imaginary letters summoned an actual letter. I received this from Jerry today:

Jacob,

*You really need to come back to Los Angeles. Why not?
What happened to you? I found your brother listed in
the phonebook and called him up. He told me you came
down with a desert fever. Really? Come on. Leave New
York before summer strikes in full. Did you catch that
movie about the locomotive boom? Just my thing—we
could make up something in that style in two days I bet
you, with the help of coffee and grilled cheese. I'm not
going to wait much longer for you though. I'm at the
Hotel Carmel in Santa Monica. Don't bother respond-
ing to this letter. If you're not knocking at my door smiling by June 15, I'll assume you're never coming back.
So come on—*

Jerry

So it's take it or leave it, a real ultimatum. I guess
Jerry's right, we could write something pretty funny about
a concrete spill on the highway or some terrible door in-
stallation mishap, any old thing in the style of the locomotive movie (a basic slapstick whose structure I bet any
college educated louse could mimic). Just the two of us in
the lobby of the Hotel Carmel, working the thing out like
naturals. Intuition!

I went to the Montreal Barber, in the downstairs arcade of the Cities Service Building in Lower Manhattan, to have a crew cut today. Afterwards, walking through the winding, narrow streets of the financial district with so little hair and a brisk wind blowing in from the Atlantic, I got quite chilly and hustled down into the Bowling Green subway station to board an uptown Lexington Avenue express. I wanted to surprise my grandfather with a lunchtime visit. Sadly, the train stalled in the tunnel between the Fulton Street and Brooklyn Bridge stations for about twenty minutes, and I experienced a deep panic. The fairly empty train quickly assumed the atmosphere of a harshly lit and absurdly spacious plastic coffin, and staring at my reflection in the doorway glass I saw my watercolor ghost. A blue light bulb in the tunnel cast a glow inside his left ear, and this served to x-ray his head and reveal a set of pink and green teeth hanging like rotten skin from brown and pimpled gums.

I came to and walked the length of the car back and forth; an old lady knitting a shirt rolled her bespectacled eyes at me, and a khaki-suited banker reading the *Sun* shook his head and muttered something I took to be: "Stop fucking idiot stop sit Jesus moron subway tonight Christ tomorrow right-now." But I continued my mad walk in the hopes that my own legs would somehow propel the train, and eventually we did start to move, and I had worked up quite a sweat and my esophagus throbbed, making it hard to swallow even what little was left of my own spittle. I got out at Brooklyn Bridge and walked home, staring down at the wood slat pedestrian walkway (catching glimpses of the river flashing below) the whole way across. I'll have to postpone the visit to my grandfather's. Maybe my aunt can drive me over there sometime soon.

The experience on the subway really exhausted me but I didn't feel like going to bed last night so I bought a crate of Coca-Cola from the Pineapple Street Grocery around 8 o'clock in the evening and drank six bottles through the night. It's now 7 o'clock in the morning and I'm yet to hit the sack. Sometime in the middle of the night I became very excited and took the jar of instant coffee that my brother gave me down from the small mantel above my bed and threw it at the wall. So now there is a pile of harsh brown sand in the southwest corner of my room, in addition to the peanut shells scattered all around.

Sitting amongst this squalor, I suddenly recall a poster I saw in a hamburger café around Santa Monica Boulevard and 26th that announced *"TRY OUR NEW HAMBURGER PEPPER LOAF TODAY!"* Hamburger pepper loaf—it has a nice ring to it, but now when I picture the food, a soggy brick of spiced ground round cooked rare, served on a paper plate overwhelmed by the density of the leaking meal, I lose my appetite.

I think I will open an impromptu hamburger stand on our stoop. Maybe I'll stroll over to the hardware store on Montague Street in a couple of hours and buy a big red and white striped beach umbrella, cook up some patties, and set up shop this evening. It's Friday, and the drunken couples strolling to the waterfront will likely give in to the temptation.

My aunt, with pronounced reluctance and disgust, agreed to drive me over to my grandfather's. In an act of passive hostility she drove an extraordinarily roundabout and pothole riddled route through Brooklyn into Queens (the Williamsburg and Greenpoint neighborhoods had apparently experienced a great chemical fire the night before, and many of the synagogues, churches, and warehouses had been reduced to black and blue crutches) and used the Queensboro Bridge to enter Manhattan. The rainy and thick gray mid-afternoon sky filled me with a great lethargy, and I nearly asked my aunt to forget about continuing uptown, she had better just drop me off at the Karen Horney psychiatric clinic that greeted us as we swung off the bridge and slammed onto the pavement of 62nd street. But I stopped myself, and instead, noticing a Chinese takeout restaurant, the Fantasy Wok Palace, I proposed that we stop for a plate of cold noodles with sesame sauce, and maybe even some mixed dumplings. My aunt shook her head and said, "Looking rather fat, you are, young man, let's better hold off on that now. Besides, I'm sure your grandfather will be spoiling you with cold cuts, butter rolls, and lemonade."

There were no cold cuts and butter rolls, but there were bottles of beer and a tray of pretzel rods. And sitting in the dining room at the long pinewood table, enjoying the beer and pretzels, I asked my grandfather if he had ever been to Los Angeles. "Well sure," he told me, "when your great-grandmother was still alive, a long time ago. It was a different place then—really just a musician's town, and I rode out there with a musician in fact, a fellow by the name of Timothy Q. Dorothy, a Dixie style drummer. He had some summer employment with a nightclub band out there, and when I saw a poster tacked to the cork board in the mailbox room of this very building that read something like 'Looking for trip companion to Los Angeles to share driving and gasoline expenses. See Timothy Dorothy in apartment 12G ASAP if interested,' I went knocking on his door right away, and we made arrangements to leave three days hence. We drove non-stop, switching shifts at the wheel every ten hours, and all we had for food was a great big pail full of sweet corn and several pounds of raisins. I spent that whole summer in Los Angeles, living in a bungalow off Pico Boulevard somewhere in the middle of town. I believe I saw Charlie Chaplin washing his car with a tremendous purple blanket once, and he wasn't wearing any shirt. I tried to break into the night-club scene there myself, as a comic, but it didn't work out and come September I was on the train back to New York City. Why, are you thinking of going?" He must have forgotten I ventured there in April—he's gotten quite senile with certain things.

I had a long dream about Hollywood last night. I found myself just beyond the entrance to Paramount Studios, standing alone under a stone white archway marked Writers' Building along the top—but the archway led to no such building, no building at all. Several policemen came through this archway and tipped their caps at me as they passed. Then my mother appeared and offered me a sardine from a can. I finished this snack and she said: "Well, we had better be on our way to the fabric outlet now, Jacob. We're needing new drapes."

But next we stood in a windswept hotel lobby with dark green and midnight blue marble floors and black velvet couches. Charlie Chaplin was sitting alone at one of the couches, smoking a pipe and reading a magazine with *Sinatra!* printed diagonally in red letters down the cover.

I stepped outside and stared into the blonde hills, bought a cup of coffee from a newsstand, and next thing I knew I was sitting in a barbershop getting a shave.

"The actress is listed. Exit off Highland and go through the cross," the barber murmured into my ear. "Her apartment building is the Egyptian style one, past the telephone print ad, ahead of the mountain range. Use the cab parked outside. Tell the driver to take you to the Vine address, he'll understand."

Then evening fell, and I was sitting alone in the back of a limousine headed for the valley. We rode uphill, and suddenly a new flat city spread out below and blasted the windshield with white light.

Suppose I stole my grandfather's gun? I just might need it when I'm back in Los Angeles. My memory of nighttime in the city is that it's extremely quiet, and the difference between a proper street and an alleyway is never altogether clear. I just don't know what I will encounter upon my return, and the more I think about Jerry the more I think he's actually a dangerous person, probably armed himself. I can see us having a draw towards the end of the afternoon on Ocean Avenue, and the notion does not strike me as completely crazy. Who knows? Anything is possible out there. I have a key to my grandfather's apartment, the doormen always let me up without any questions—and he mentioned something about a doctor's appointment on Wednesday morning. I'll slip in then. I'm not going to make it to LA before the June 15th deadline set by Jerry, but better late than never. And a belated arrival will startle him anyway, giving me a much-needed leg up in our relations.

That was simple. Inside the big ceramic white jar marked Cotton, underneath a generous layer of cotton balls, I retrieved my grandfather's gun—just a stub of a pistol that fits nicely in the inside pocket of my khaki summer coat. It's fully loaded, I opened the cylinder to see. Then I headed to Penn Station and bought a ticket to LA. I'm in no rush and the train is cheaper. I leave in two days. I haven't let my brother know I'm heading out. I'll just call him when I'm there. Having a gun makes me slightly nervous. I think I will pack it wedged among my socks and underpants. I certainly don't want it in my pocket as I ride the train; it would affect my behavior while I share a dining table with a passenger, and I don't want to raise any suspicions. I'm just a young man on the train to Los Angeles, minding my own business, willing to chat if you wish. My gun is up on the luggage rack, but only I know that, and I already forgot it's there.

I'm all settled in my sleeper car and in a moment I'll head to the dining car for supper. After cleaning my room of the mess I'd made on the floor and saying goodbye to my mother and aunt (such sad, frail creatures the two of them; the three of us hugged in a group, huddled like some pathetically outnumbered badminton squad, but I'm sure they're enjoying an evening smoke on the stoop now, better off in the end without my noises and moods) I hailed a cab which whisked me to Penn Station. I'm ready to go—I'm going.

It's the middle of the night and we're somewhere in or around Ohio, passing the occasional wooden or aluminum shed in an otherwise empty landscape. We could be passing graveyards too but I wouldn't know. It's so dark outside and the light in my room casts a glare on the window so nothing stands out in the country except these sagging sheds with triangular reflectors pasted to their roofs and doors. I brought the 1860 *Leaves of Grass* along with me, and I've been flipping through it, wondering if there could be some way to adapt Whitman's material into a script— say, a cowboy version of "Crossing Brooklyn Ferry." I'm almost ashamed to have that idea, but it's such ideas, I think, that sell: crooked ideas, Hollywood prisms . . .

I've been languishing in my compartment, working on some more of these letters to and from Los Angeles. I guess I could write a real letter to my mother and aunt and a postcard to my grandfather too to tell them about the train trip, but there's really not much to report. The train moves slowly. I see the country turn into a desert.

Steve,

I've been sitting in the director's yard all day. Bo is in the library most days studying. I will have to meet you later this month to discuss the termination of business —all of our cameras got stuck. Hence, I send this note with some regret, and hope that you haven't bought a house out here yet.

Regards,

Dan

Sammy,

Why'd you say that about me being a Missourian for life? You know I'm no homebody. I'm in Santa Fe. I'm in the West for sure now, and headed your way. I think I'll dye my hair black in the kitchen sink. There are so many fleas here. Another thought: I'll marry that Susan I told you about, but wait until next year, once I'm established in a cutting room. Then I'll send for her.

Your friend,

Freddy

Gregg,

I drank a beer this morning, a light beer, very refreshing. And I have a water fountain in my back yard. Everything is ready for you. Have I ever told you I have

a lot of faith in you? I do. I intend to die here someday,
so—right, grow a chinstrap beard, buy a car, and trust
in the Lord that everything will be just fine. Because you
know everything is just fine.

    Take it easy,
    Joshua

I have a feeling I'll meet some of these Steves, Dans, Sammys, Freddys, Greggs, and Joshuas when I settle in Los Angeles, so I may as well get to know them a little bit now. This is preparatory work I'm doing.

I arrived at the Hotel Carmel By the Sea (whose damp lobby bore the surprising mixed scent of daisies, dog turd, and milk-soaked corn flakes) a sweaty mess in brown sunglasses, and headed straight to the desk and asked the ravishing young lady in a blue sailor's cap for Mr. Jerry Stamp's room number. To my chagrin, and I'm still recovering now, she gave me the news that there's no Mr. Jerry Stamp staying at the Carmel, nor has a Mr. Jerry Stamp ever been a guest at the Carmel since she started here four months ago. A mother with a screeching baby strung to her neck by some cotton hammock was waiting for her turn behind me, and this noise combined with the realization that the smell of dog turd had just been overthrown by the warm one of infant diarrhea, plus the fact of Jerry's absence, not to mention the confused exhaustion brought on by several days spent on the cross-country train—all of this and more (like the fat, red-in-the-face tuxedoed old man playing an accordion and singing "A Gay Caballero" in the doorway) made me very thirsty for a beer, and I went along Broadway a ways but couldn't find a bar, so I've been sitting on this bench on Ocean Avenue staring at the Pacific Ocean, trying to collect my thoughts and muster up the courage to call my brother and tell him that, basically, I am stranded in Santa Monica.

After about three hours of dawdling on the bench and occasionally looking over at a couple of old ladies playing chess on a concrete table, I called my brother from a booth on California Avenue outside the post office and we had a fairly decisive conversation:

—*What are you doing here*, he asked.

—*I don't know. I thought Jerry was here and that we'd work together.*

—*Well?*

—*Well it turns out he's not here and I don't know if he ever was here.*

—*So what are you going to do?*

—*Well, I'm here, aren't I?*

—*Cats.*

—*Cats?*

—*What? So what are you going to do?*

—*I suppose I don't know.*

—*Well, transform.*

—*Transform?*

—*Jacob? What is this—come on then, so what will you do, where will you live? I know a building on Wilshire, quite far from the ocean—what do you think of that?*

—*Sure.*

—*O.K., how do I get a hold of you once I've set this up?*

—*I'll just call you tomorrow night, O.K.?*

—*Fine, call me at 7.*

I spent last night at the Hotel Carmel. I don't think I slept at all. The room came furnished with a radio, and I listened to the country music station all night, which mostly played Patsy Cline songs I'd never heard before, and I had terrible visions of the great singer being forced around by a gang of studio technicians. The one terrible thought kept running through my head: She probably recorded those songs in Hollywood and got raped at the end of every session. I had a cold fear in my gut that lasted until the sun came up and then I found a deli where I drank an excess of coffee and water and consumed a small bowl of complimentary coleslaw.

My brother picked me up in front of the Carmel around 8 o'clock at night and we drove a long ways east on Wilshire, past the university, past Beverly Hills, and into a neighborhood that resembles 5th Avenue in Midtown Manhattan. We didn't talk much during the drive, and the road was empty save for the stray fruit and vegetable truck zooming west. My brother seemed quite angry with me as he clenched the wheel and repeatedly asked about "this Jerry"—"So what is going on with this Jerry?" and

"But who is this Jerry anyway?" I couldn't come up with any answers, except to say that, basically, he's an acquaintance from New York with whom I intend to write scripts, but I don't know what's become of him. We stopped at a red light and he shook his head. "Well Jacob, you're going to have to come up with a new plan now. You must adapt."

We passed a big Neo-Gothic cathedral that looked like St. Patrick's and then I expected to see Saks Fifth Avenue and hot dog and pretzel vendors, but as we passed on to the next block my brother stopped the car in front of a tall brown building. "This is it," he said, "The Strutter Arms. Wait in the car." I watched him have a quick exchange with the desk attendant, and then he pulled me out of the car and escorted me up to my room on the 15th floor.

"I'll pay your rent the first month while you get on your feet," he said. "But you'd better work. Look, you've got what you need now—bed, desk, sink, window—so I'll be going."

I told him there was no need for him to pay my rent, the money father left behind would hold me over, but he insisted. I almost proposed that we have a beer in the pub connected to the lobby (I noticed a padded leather door marked Strutter's Pub on our way to the elevator), but I couldn't even catch his eye, so I just thanked him as he walked out and sat down on the springy bed.

Looking around outside this morning I discovered that The Strutter Arms is on Kingsley Drive, and across the way I found a grocery store where I bought a bag of corn chips, a cup of sour cream, and a bottle of red wine. I just finished these things, my lunch, and I'm looking out the window down at the street lined with banks, piano dealers, haberdashers, costume shops, and Mexican restaurants. My pants smell badly of stale sweat and I think I should find a Laundromat. But first I need to decide where to store my grandfather's pistol. Will it be in one of the dresser drawers, or maybe there's a trapdoor behind the map of Utah that hangs on the wall?

I see: there is no trapdoor. It's a shame this desk doesn't have any drawers, shelves, or any style of compartments whatsoever—it's actually just a square black and white tile table jutting out of the wall next to the sink, with a stool connected to it by a steel pipe coming out from the side and making a rather awkward maneuver of three right angles in the air to arrive at an appropriate enough spot below and before the desk. You can spin around on the wooden stool seat. I suppose it was once some sort of vanity table, but I feel like I'm sitting at the counter in an underground Liverpool milk bar, and I'm reminded of the beginning of Melville's *White Jacket*: "I employed myself, for several days, in manufacturing an outlandish garment of my own devising, to shelter me from the boisterous weather we were soon to encounter." Those must be the exact words proclaimed by the builder of this desk as he examined the floor and wall and danced around in a mess of plaster, steel, and black and white tile. Oh that I could eat a doughnut with Herman Melville in Los Angeles! To the Laundromat!

These past few days I have tried to get to work, as my brother instructed me. But I cannot concentrate. It might have something to do with the tile desk, which is so uncomfortable; the stool puts me at an awkward height (I actually must reach up to write), and the deep grooves on the writing surface, due to the cavernous gaps between tiles, make me restless. So I attempted to work in the lobby, which is furnished with some corduroy couches and glass coffee tables. But I experienced no luck down there, and I thought about going to Union Station where I could sit in a dark corner next to a potted tree and take notes on the travelers, loiterers, and sandwich-makers. The daytime attendant here at the Strutter spends most of his time on the telephone discussing the stock market in a grating, goose-like tone. "How's my GE shaking, Rodney?" he asks every twenty minutes. And when he's not on the line he eats bologna and mayonnaise sandwiches, smacking his lips with such abandon that the sound ricochets off the high tin ceiling and clacks in my own ear like degraded horse hoofs hitting wet pavement. This building disagrees with me, but I must try to focus and keep up a positive mindset. The sun does not seem to shine much in this neighborhood, though; the overcast sky and the faded yellow and white palm trees depress me.

Where is Jerry? No more ignoring the issue. I've got to find him. Meanwhile I am yet to do the laundry, instead inserting my coins into the jukebox at the pub, where I drink coke and look out the window: Twice I thought I saw Jerry, but it was just the postman at the beginning and end of his rounds.

I approached the obnoxious daytime attendant and asked him how I might go about discovering a person in this town. "Discovering a person how?" he asked me, with a speck of dried mayonnaise stuck to his thin black moustache. Well then, I made myself clear, and told him: "I am looking for a man named Jerry Stamp. I was supposed to meet him at the Hotel Carmel, over in Santa Monica. But the Carmel told me Jerry Stamp never checked in to the hotel. Still, I know he's in Los Angeles somewhere." He asked what makes me so sure that he's here, and I suppose that's a reasonable question.

"This is one big city and I don't know what to tell you son," he quacked at me as he dialed a number on the phone.

I walked downtown to the Central Library today, a long walk of at least four miles. On my way, I resolved to carry on in Los Angeles despite the fact that Jerry is missing. I found a carrel in a corner next to a courtyard-facing window and settled down with a library copy of Melville's *Mardi*. "But whence, and whither wend ye, mariners?" Lost in the first chapter and pleased with the indoor sunshine and odor of books, I suddenly felt a tap on my shoulder. I looked up and there was Jerry, the slippery goon himself.

Tanned and wearing a freshly pressed gray linen suit, he playfully patted me on the cheek. "I knew I'd find you here, you sad sack. What's this hooloomooloo you're reading?" He spoke at a volume far too loud for a library, well above a whisper and just below a bellow. "Come on, let's go have a sandwich in Pershing Square and talk things out."

Apparently, Jerry is living in Hollywood above a hamburger joint near Paramount Studios. "I never checked in to the Carmel. Just wanted to throw you off—it's good to be thrown off, you must have that experience here, it gets the creative juices flowing."

I suppose.

"Anyway, I'm working on a script about a marching band, a college-based comedy, and one of the assistant directors who frequents the burger joint assured me he'd take a look once I'm finished. Trouble is, I can't seem to wrap it up. Care to give me a hand with the ending?"

I told him I didn't know, and he laughed and asked what could be the matter with me. Then we got in his yellow convertible and drove along Melrose Avenue a ways, and ended up—as he informed me—in the Bel Air district. We made several fast laps around a slanted and dark tree-lined track, something like the loop in Central Park, but decidedly more modern. I asked him how he got the car. "They give them away here like soup, Jacob; I told the dealer I'm a screenwriter closing in on a deal with Paramount, and that was proof enough for him that I'm in good credit."

When he finally dropped me off at the Strutter he told me I'd better move in with him, because we've got a lot of work to do, and money to make.

There's a synagogue nearby, the Wilshire Temple. I went in this morning. I hadn't set foot in a synagogue since the memorial service for my father. The domed ceiling provided a sudden shift in orientation, perhaps because the Los Angeles sky lacks curve. Here, the sky lies so high above, flat like slate, and never bends.

After a few minutes of gazing stupidly upwards, I stepped outside and a hunched, skinny old man wearing a torn cabbie's woolen hat waved his cane at me and made wild accusations. "They build the temple, and now you kids think you can come rattle in and just keep going, hey? Quit this shaking the movies. Ever heard of paying dues, cretin?"

I tried to move along but I brushed against the old man's cable sweater, which seemed to be devoid of limbs, and mumbled sorry. "Don't call me sonny!" he yelled.

"I didn't call you sonny," I offered, "I merely said sorry. I am sorry I bumped into you."

"You young movie shits," he growled back at me. "Go back to Miami," he finished.

I hurried on and moved around the blocks in several directions, losing track, and ended up on a street called Fedora, where I leaned against a dumpster and smoked a cigarette—the first I've had, actually, since returning to town. It tasted nice and sweet, like fresh strawberry dirt, and I considered Jerry's offer. Live with him in Hollywood? Perhaps. Why not?

I phoned my brother from a Strutter booth and let him know I'd run into Jerry at the Central Library and that I think I'll move in with him so we can get to work on scripts. "You think so? What about that month's rent I paid? You think it means nothing to me? You think I wanted you to throw it away for me? Thanks then. Fine, move along. But I've got no more favors for you. You're a brat, just like mother. You have none of father's drive— you're lazy and weak. Good luck, shit." Now I've been called a shit twice in one day.

My brother never really wanted me out here anyway, so this is good, I've effectively severed our connection. I suspect, even, that he sabotaged my first attempt to live here. Yes, he sickened me somehow, snuck into my Santa Monica room and lightly poisoned my bedside glass of water with a bizarre and flavorless extract of his flowers.

Still in the booth, I dashed off a few short missives between the imaginary and unknown:

Hey Gregg,

Up in the hills with the young trees. I'll show you. Why not? I say: you'd like it up here, even better than my old place. Live and learn, as they say in Monterey.

Best,

Joshua

P.S. Lots of murders in town—really makes you want to get out and see!

Sammy,

I'm telling you, this will bowl you over. I met with a lounge singer last night. He told me he'd get me a meeting with his manager, who also works with some of the top cutters. Fingers crossed. When are you going to leave Pasadena and come closer to the action, you jerk?

In good stead, instead of anything else—and just because,

Freddy

"Welcome to the Hollywood Dump!" yelled Jerry as he pulled me into his place and gave me a great long bear hug. The burger joint Jerry lives above is called the Olive Pit. The acrid stink of grease seeps up through his floor and fills the room. I nearly choked at first. It's a dirty place consisting of several folding wooden chairs (most of them folded up and leaning against the walls, though some of them have crashed to the floor and lie in uneven piles), a couple of bridge tables pushed into the corners, and three oversized white couches stained with coffee. The floor is littered with television magazines, receipts from liquor stores, movie ticket stubs, and scraps of torn up pages. There are windows on all sides, so the place is flooded with sunlight. "Some cocaine?" he asked as he unfolded a chair for me and placed it in the middle of the room. I declined and noticed a lit burner on the stove. I pointed this out and he rushed over in a flurry of laughter to turn it off.

"You can sleep on any of the couches, it doesn't matter to me, really," he said. "They're all the same, really! Throw your baggage anyplace, and let's get to work. The assistant director shows up at the Pit every Friday around ten at night for a snack, so we've got two days to work out this ending. The basic idea is, it's the University of Chicago marching band, and they're terrible. But then this beautiful freshman girl joins the band, and she's a genius trumpet player, and all of the boys want her. We want to suggest, though, that she's a hermaphrodite—but we can never be at all explicit about this, we must just keep it between you and me and work on the audience in a purely subliminal manner. It's a psychological plot crux, or crutch, or what have you. One fellow, a particular dweeb, a stereotypical Chicago boy always carrying *Wealth of Nations* wedged up in his arm-pit—one of the bass drummers—he's the one who gets her alone one spring night on the Midway, behind the Fountain of Time statue. But here, read it. Like I said, what we've got to figure out is the ending, the last scene."

I'd never heard Jerry so excited, but I accepted his fervor and found it rather contagious. I sat down on a couch and read, and I must say, I was quite impressed. I'd never read a script before, but this material had me gripped from the opening scene, which has the band sitting in a hall at the university's International House listening to an esteemed military band leader deliver a scolding lecture on the five points every marching band member must know, and somehow the whole situation blistered with suspense.

A fairly embarrassing incident this morning. Jerry must have gone through my bags in the middle of the night. "Interesting old prop gun you have there in your main sack, friend." What did he mean, prop gun?

"It even has little metal plugs cemented in to look like bullets when you release the cylinder. Nifty."

I went along with it, though. "Yes," I smiled, "I thought you'd get a kick out of it. Maybe we should stage a hold up of the Olive Pit."

"Hell no! The owner of the place is a friendly Greek but he has absolutely no sense of humor and he'd probably kill us the moment he sees one of us flash a gun, fake or no—he wouldn't know." He threw the gun at me. I pointed and shot at the ceiling. Indeed, it just made a quiet click, no louder than a handheld attendance counter, and ejected no bullet. I forced out a chuckle and suggested that we go outside to find some breakfast.

We walked along Van Ness a ways, passed the great Hollywood Memorial Park Cemetery, and bought some coffee, little bags of cereal, and a bunch of grapes, from a cart also selling star maps.

We determined two options for how to end the script: either violently or romantically. We went with the latter. The girl falls for the dweeb and they drive to New York and board a Cunard ship bound for England, with plans to start up the Overseas American College Century Band. The final scene has the two performing on the deck—she blowing a Gypsy tune and he keeping time with his thumping bass drum—and a group of children begin an impromptu dance party under a crescent moon as the ship sails through the Atlantic evening.

Jerry went down to the Olive Pit a little while ago to hand the script over to the assistant director. I imagine he's just hyping the thing up for a bit and that he'll return any minute now. It's nearly midnight.

It's morning and Jerry hasn't come upstairs. I found a cat sleeping on a western-facing window ledge. She's black except for her legs and paws, which are white with spots of light brown. I've given her a bit of vanilla pudding that I found in Jerry's fridge behind the cans of beer, lemons, and moldy bricks of cheddar cheese.

Still no trace of Jerry. I can't stop thinking about the ocean. Perhaps I can find a bus on Santa Monica Boulevard that will take me all the way west. The stinking hamburger and French fry grease gives me a hellish headache. I wonder if Jerry keeps another apartment someplace. I named the cat Sam.

I left Jerry a note, should he come back today, telling him that I went to spend the day at the ocean and that I'll be back this evening. I waited in front of a 76 gas station on Santa Monica Boulevard and La Brea and after about an hour I went into the mechanic's shop to ask how often the bus comes. "On Sundays it comes only twice," a cover-alled man lying on his back underneath an army jeep shouted. "Noon and six." Well, I must have just missed the noon. So now I'm back in the Hollywood Dump, chasing dust balls around the room with Sam and reading her bits of the 1860 *Leaves of Grass*.

"This night I am happy; / As I walk the beach where the old mother sways to / and fro, singing her savage and husky song, / As I watch the stars shining—I think a thought of / the clef of the universes, and of the future."

I found a dilapidated upright piano on the curb this morning. I asked the Greek at the Olive Pit if he knew the story. "It's garbage crap," he told me. "One of the boys cleaning the cellar last night found it behind the cans of tomato paste and relish. Take it away."

I gave the dishwasher three dollars to help me carry it upstairs. We put it down against the wall next to the bathroom. "Enjoy this," he said, "it's not all the time you can find a loose instrument and have it like this." I told him I would, thanked him for his help, and offered him a glass of water. He declined, wiping his hands together. "I have a pile of dishes to attend to always, it is growing bigger. Have a good day!"

The piano is out of tune, some of the keys don't work, and it sounds like cheap bells. But I like it. I've never taken a piano lesson, but I can bang out melodies. My father hated when I did this. He knew how to play the piano —he liked to struggle with Bach's fugues and Chopin's nocturnes—and couldn't stand me sitting there producing what he called Chinese parlor nonsense. "Get away from there," he would say, "please stop playing that insulting music, I need to practice."

I set a bowl of cottage cheese on top of the piano (I bought a few things at the 76 station shop around midnight last night) and Sam sat up there eating and when she finished she sprawled out on her side as I played.

Around 3 in the afternoon Jerry returned and dropping a large brown shopping bag overflowing with *Variety* magazines on the floor he said, "Keep playing Stan," even though that's not my name, "I'm in the mood to sing." So I kept playing my choppy, redundant melodies and for two hours Jerry sang along a string of mad lyrics.

First, he sang of "chewing a flavorless stick o' gum on

the autobahn to Vegas." Then, in a mock-whisper, and tip-toeing in circles around the room he sang about "smoking a little pipe, I'm a Jesuit nurse I am." Next he screamed, "I found a song, dick, and it broke!" over and over again, at least one hundred times. He took a brief break and opened each of us a can of beer. After a few gulps he drew circles in the air with his index finger pointed at me and I resumed playing as he chirped "I sure wish my cabin was a sub-marine" and "I'm sitting here in London with my daughter named Sue" and "I'm sitting at my desk wishing it was you." Then he belted out a series of songs with the same chorus: "Take a right on the turn-pike grandpa, take a meal in Kentucky now, Kentucky fried Susan, well dontcha come on back to me!" He ended with a 25-minute Irish-inflected lament, mostly whining that "I've got the rickets, dear wife, well I've got the rick-ets once again."

Then he lay down on a couch and passed out. He's been sleeping there for five hours now.

Jerry woke me up this morning by dumping the bag of *Variety* on my head, and I have bruises on my forehead and cheeks now.

I asked him what happened with the assistant director. "He never showed up." Then I asked him, where's the script? "I lost it climbing up the graveyard wall in my attempt to get over into Paramount."

"I had it wedged in back of my pants-waist you see. Suddenly it slips out, falls into a thick rosebush, and disappears." Did he get into Paramount? Of course not: "A cemetery guard beamed in on me with his damned flashlight."

"So I climbed down and they put me away in a den in their administrative tower these past few days. They have their own kind of private jail there, you could say. I was forced to organize by date all of the overseer's *Variety* magazines, and compose an annotated catalogue. At least I did such a good job that he let me come away with all these duplicates."

I woke up very early this morning, around 7 o'clock, and the overcast sky put me in a strong mood for vegetable soup. Luckily I found a 24-hour wok not too far away on Vine and ordered one—clear broth, yellow noodles, bamboo shoots, broccoli, and snow peas—and settled down in the outdoor café, under an umbrella because of the drizzle. Jerry was still asleep when I left. I don't feel like going back to the Dump anytime soon.

After the soup I made my way over to a brownstone throne in the courtyard at the Egyptian Theatre, and considered three options: call my brother, see a movie, or find a bus to Las Vegas. I decided that the middle option is the safest, but remained on the throne.

At least the sun is out now and I can hear the traffic moving along Hollywood Boulevard. Now that the day is underway, I must take action. I realize I can combine the brotherly and Vegas options: my brother ventures to the desert about once a month on business. I know from the letters he sent me in New York that he supplies one of the new hotel-casinos with all of its floral decorations, and also advises the management on how and where to place all of the arrangements in the lobbies, guest rooms, game spaces, lounges, and rest rooms. Maybe he's due for another trip and I could come along, assuming he's no longer furious with me.

After another hour or so in the courtyard, I got up and walked over to the Fairfax Farmers Market. I followed the instructions given to me by the girl in the box office and took Highland south to Melrose, then Melrose west to Fairfax, and finally Fairfax south to 3rd. Now I'm sitting in one of the dining patios, imitating the hero of *Brass Rain*—eating a doughnut, drinking coffee from a Styrofoam cup, and taking notes. It's been a while since I wrote any Los Angeles letters, so I'm working on those. I hear the gentlemen hawking turkey burgers and pizza bread and frosted cinnamon rolls all around me. The smell of freshly pressed waffle cones keeps me on my toes.

> *Jack,*
> *Hello, old friend. I've owed you a letter some while now.*
> *Sorry to be out of touch. I've been feeling down and*

*fallen way behind. I miss the Staten Island Ferry and
my work lofts, my paintbrushes, and my many Chinese
girlfriends. If only I had a house on the Palisades and
a great-grandma to take care of me. But I live next to
a Local Loan outlet in the back of Hollywood, and I tell
you soon enough it will be me lining up and humming
gospel songs while I wait. 1946 is a tough year for me,
Jack. And how about you? Are you still on 38th and
8th, working at the Center of the World Restaurant?
How are tips? They still give waiters free hot dogs for
lunch? How's the wife? I finally have some advice for
you. Don't ever move to Southern California. So maybe
I'm a little wiser now at least. O.K. I'm going to go find
a cowboy extra in the street and maybe beat him up with
a broomstick, or at least taunt him with it. Take care of
yourself—*

    Carl

It's probably just the coffee and sugar that's making me
feel agitated, but I'm shaking around at the moment. I'll
find a drinking fountain. I think I hear a pair of journal-
ists behind me discussing the story of the land next door,
where CBS now stands:

—*First the oil field, then the football field.*

—*But also the donkey baseball.*

—*Dog shows.*

—*And rodeos.*

—*Boxing.*

—*I tell you I like the Television City beat.*

—*Me too.*

—*Well, better get back to work.*

—*Yep. I'm sitting in on Twilight Zone this afternoon.*

—*I'm headed to Video Village.*

—*Take care Simpson.*

—*Take care Johnson.*

I smell jasmine in the air, a thick stench like fresh bub-
blegum. It fills my nostrils and makes me want to sit in
the Atlantic harbor and take in the smell of my native sea.
The Pacific smells of nothing, it has no cleanse. It only
produces air, no odor, and does nothing to counteract the
jasmine.

From Fairfax and 3rd, I took a cab to Santa Monica and

went looking for my Parker Jotter. But I couldn't even find the old apartment building where I came down with that hellish fever.

I walked a ways down Ocean Avenue and turned down Pico to the sea and came upon the majestic sandstone Hotel Ross and considered blowing what remains of my inheritance by staying in one of their suites. Eating breakfast in the lobby while staring at the sea, meeting an actress, marrying her, going into severe debt; then she leaves me, so I become a bellhop at the Ross.

I spent the night at a motel on Main Street, thinking over this plan, and right now it doesn't sound like such a terrible way to proceed. Better yet, I can skip those preliminary steps and cross straight over to the bellhop stage.

First, I withdrew the rest of my money and used it to buy a sharp apple-green suit—baggy in the shoulders, and a pleated front to the pant. I chose a seemingly subdued black and brown tie (with a touch of yellow); a closer inspection, though, reveals the illustration of a thick haired and smiling ape face. I wanted to emerge from this process with precisely $50 in my pocket and there was plenty more than that leftover still, so I walked over to the Santa Monica Pier and stuffed the excess bills in a pair of blue and white striped athletic socks that I bought with the suit, and threw my inheritance into the calm afternoon water. Some lucky bather will find it.

I took a ride on the Ferris wheel, and now it's off to the Hotel Ross to inquire after any openings.

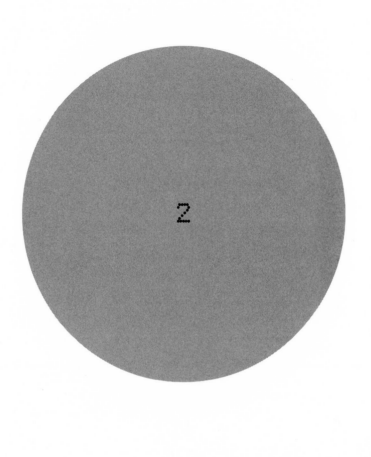

AS BELLHOP NUMBER SIX I LIVE
in the eastern staff quarters in my own tiny windowless
room, which looks like it was previously a private sauna
—all soft and faded wooden walls.

I work the 2 to 10 p.m. shift. I must take my lunch before reporting to duty. I've just been to the icebox next to
my bed where I removed two pieces of brown Wonder
Bread, fetched a can of diced ham and a jar of horserad-
ish mustard from the crate under my bed, and prepared
a sandwich. It all felt surprisingly difficult, yet deeply
meaningful.

On my late-afternoon half-hour break I climb the fire
escape to the roof of the Ross and turn my back on the sea
and throw white stones down at the kitchen dumpsters in
the alley. I like the noise of stone hitting metal.

I wonder what Jerry's done with all the things in my
bags—my clothes, my toothpicks, spare buttons, decks of
cards, sunglasses, and that supposed prop gun. Perhaps
I could send him a postcard and ask him to bring it all to

Disney Land to give to Snow White and tell her it's from me. But he wouldn't do me the favor. He would seduce her and take her behind a castle and pull up her skirt.

Sometimes, I admit, I do look at the ocean when I'm on the roof. It's hard not to. And sometimes I look over at the bluffs of Malibu. And recently when I looked out I fell asleep standing up (something I never thought would happen to me) and I dreamed I was driving my mother along the coastal highway. We stopped along the way to buy the New York and Los Angeles newspapers, as well as some various bottles of fruit-flavored soda (grape, orange, green lemon), and then we put these things in the trunk and continued on.

We got to Malibu in the middle of the afternoon and found a nice bench on a cliff where we read the papers and drank the soda until it got dark. The nighttime put me in a negative and agitated mood, and I began to worry about money and uttered, "How can you swear by the bank? If you had a choice between some Doric column in the ladies room and the palm tree covering the banker's face, what would you choose?"

She froze and gave me a worried, terrified stare. I stood up and raised a golf club in the air and shouted: "I'm talking about the garage. The men who sit in front of it—you know what they did with father and you need to tell me about it."

I was all set to smash her skull with the golf club when I awoke with the dire need to urinate.

Dear Steele,

I will write letters only to you now. I discarded my address book, the one with all the big names in it. It's true what you say, that people do not know what you're thinking, but can always tell what you're feeling.

I am an actress. That's what I do. I wear hats. I'm doing fantastic, actually. I look down the beach and see gasoline in the air, so it's like I'm looking at everything through a piece of wet glass. Should I give up smoking? All of the other actresses do it.

I am having a re-birth, over and over again. I never feel sleepy, never ever never! Little palms and big palms and purple dates smashed into the pavement and I fall in love. Then I fail. I don't know, truly, what the place is doing to me, other than that I look both directions, up the hills and out to sea and I think, I am roasting with the stars, and we're all working on the same movie about a bowl of cherries and a pack of Utah lizards. They're all drunk—the director, the assistant director, the screenwriters, everyone on the lot, drunk all of the time. I don't know how anything gets done here.

And the producers ask me—me of all the women, I can't believe it, they're all more beautiful than I—to be the star of the movie. The director tells me I'm the only one. And I sleep with him. I'm totally steeped in it, but I am also so afraid that I'll be thrown out. I can't tell. I will know more soon, I hope.

Love,
Gracie

The Ross was kind enough to outfit my room with a bedside radio. I turn it on and hear the Dave Brubeck Quartet play "Take 5" and feel like punching up the steam-softened walls. I call my brother and listen in the earpiece to about five minutes of a strange harsh buzzing (much like the sound produced by those practical-joke electric shock handshake toys), and he never answers. Maybe he moved. I think of the empty shuffleboard courts outside, how they're never in use. The back of my skull vibrates, but I don't think it's anything serious. I will try my brother again. No, I will make my way without him. Anyway, that's what I'm already doing.

It occurs to me, what if I were a jobber, the kind of jobber who shuttles between Los Angeles and New York on a regular basis? A guy in Los Angeles on a job I don't really want to talk about? It's just something to do with coffee beans. I stay at the Beverly Hilton most times I'm in town. I admit I'm not such an important fellow but the overall enterprise most certainly is. What I do is, I wander the city and check on what kind of coffee beans all the delicatessens are using. I don't mind the work at all. I like to walk around the Fairfax District for instance, eating an apple and waltzing through a rusty-framed doorway and ordering a cup of coffee. And I ask nonchalantly, "What kind of coffee do you folks use? This is real good, ma'am." The waitresses always tell me; sometimes they grimace or snort at my curiosity, but nothing worse. My bosses pay me $100 a day to gather this information. It's that valuable to the New York distributors.

Why don't I want to talk about the work? Because I'm in all kinds of trouble, and this job is off the books, under the table. I'm blacklisted. I'm too old for this, too young for that. I drink gin and apple juice for lunch. I'm a Canadian Jew, also a frightened atheist. I was born in Chicago on the first of June. The bases were loaded at the bottom of the 7th. I took my chances and lighted out for the territory. Or at least my parents did. They moved down to Houston and left me in Chicago with my grandma, a heavy-set beer drinker with a beard coming on. I had a rough childhood in the 1940s, to the say the least, growing up on State Street south of the Loop, boarding in an outsize rug factory closet.

I thought up a bit of dialogue this morning, and it almost makes me miss Jerry:

> *Todd: Why doesn't she wear a brown wig?*
> *Jim: I don't know. Have you ever asked her?*
> *Todd: Heavens no, that would be rude.*

A few days ago I had a bit of an accident. I was up on the roof as usual during my break, looking around, and paying particular attention to a flock of seagulls circling the City Hall building (like a miniature United States Capitol building, but with a bunch of lanky cacti planted in a circle on the roof), when I fell off and landed feet first in an open dumpster. Luckily the dumpster had some trash bags inside—full of shrimp, judging by the smell; but the landing still sent a shock up both legs and I heard a crack and pretty soon I passed out.

Next thing I know I'm in the Ross infirmary, both my legs cast in brown plaster and elevated by slings. A nurse comes by my bed three times a day to give me some morphine and a kiss on the forehead. But she does not speak to me. She only smiles when I say hello and ask how her day is going. Her blonde curly hair smells like baby powder, and sometimes her white shirt isn't buttoned all the way up and I can steal a peak at her orange freckled bosom.

Now I'm well enough to sit in a wheelchair with my legs outstretched. The Ross has quite an elaborate health complex, it turns out, with several wards—emergency, rehabilitation, psychological, gastrointestinal, cardiac, and even a special pharmacological laboratory. I'm off the morphine now and on some milder painkiller. Those head vibrations I was experiencing before I fell are gone, and I really feel better than I have in years. I get to sit by the window with a view of the sailboats and swimmers in the Pacific, and read *Dick Tracy* comics throughout the day. No complaints. There are very few other patients in my wing (oddly I can't determine what ward I'm in—there are no signs indicating where I am, only signs pointing to all of the other units), just the stray emaciated old man lying on a bed under a ceiling window, drenched in white light, and a few young boys in a sandbox relearning how to use their hands with the help of a crew of burly men with thick black sideburns and bulbous noses, wearing long white coats with large green 'HRH' insignias stitched on the back, like an occult baseball team come to visit from another dimension.

The nurse brought me a copy of the *Sun* this morning. The headline shouts: "*UPTOWN BURNS.*"

According to the article, mysterious fires have been sweeping through the Upper East and Upper West Sides of Manhattan for the past five days. Supposedly, the only explanation is natural causes—"cloud fires"—"petroleum rain and sulfuric lightning causing a frantic organic combustion that sets rooftops ablaze and great confusion and panic in the lobbies, butcher shops, and shoe stores." Curiously, Brooklyn is fine, so I've no reason to worry about my mother and aunt, but what about my grandfather?

I wheeled myself over to a payphone and placed a collect call. "Jacob! Where've you been, you jerk?" he asked with a guffaw.

I told him I'm in Los Angeles, currently healing a pair of broken legs.

"Good for you," he sang. "You're right where you belong. My neighborhood is chaos, non-stop sirens. Have you heard about the fires?"

"That's why I'm calling, grandpa. Are you alright?"

"I'm fine," he chortled. "To tell you the truth, I like the blackened skies and orange flames sizzling down from the rooftops across the way. Don't you know I'm a bit of a grim-faced prick? I tell you, this is how I've always wanted to go down, to burn to the ground on Park Avenue, a very special kind of cremation. I'm keeping myself busy with a deck of cards and an old bottle of Swedish vodka. I've still got bread to toast, and some marmalade for the spreading, and when I run out of supplies, so it goes! Don't worry about me."

"If you say so, grandpa, all right. Well, I love you. Have fun."

"I love you too, boy. I'm real proud of you. Stick to your guns out there and get well soon. I bet you have a nice nurse there, I can hear it in your voice. Enjoy! You only live once, schmuck!"

"For sure. Thanks grandpa. Goodbye."

I took my grandfather's advice, and the next time the nurse came over to give me a cup of pills and a kiss, I took her by the hand, looked into her hazel eyes, and told her she's beautiful—the most beautiful woman I have ever seen, and really the sweetest to boot. Would she sit on my lap? She most certainly would, and she did. And she moved around gently, and her underpants became quite wet, and I began to kiss the back of her neck, and squeeze her hardened nipples with all of my fingers, and then she turned around and pulled my pajama pants down a ways and began to lick me with the tip of her tongue until I was about ready to explode, and then she stopped and standing before me with her eyes closed she began to finger herself where there wasn't any hair, and reached the point of ecstasy, and then grabbed me, and so did I, which made quite a mess on the window to the sea, which she promptly cleared away with a pink beach towel.

What can I say? Am I ashamed of this encounter? Indeed, yet I also feel relieved. Then again, I feel guilty that we've never had a conversation. But it's not my fault that she chooses to lead a speechless existence. We try to act like nothing transpired between us. She still brings me my pills and kisses me on the forehead, but that quick flash of the eyes we once exchanged is gone and her shirt is always buttoned straight up to the top now.

Yesterday a doctor knelt down and rested a hand on my thigh and chatted with me by the window. He told me the casts would be removed in two days, but that I'll have to remain in the infirmary until I'm fully healed and, as he put it, walking like a professional again.

"Fine with me," I said, "just as long as you continue renewing your stock of *Dick Tracy* comic books."

"Of course," he assured me. "Anything else?"

"Bring me a copy of the *Sun* tomorrow morning, would you? I want to keep abreast of the uptown Manhattan blaze."

"Ah, that's some event," he remarked, applying his stethoscope to his chest and appearing to listen intently to his own heartbeat. "Certainly, young man. We will keep you informed."

Where are the damned doctors? It's been six days now and I'm just sitting here bound in my casts growing crusty at the mouth from this regimen of pills. I told the nurse I think it's high time they lower the dosage or change the prescription, for no amount of water seems to slake my thirst and I'm feeling dizzy and sad throughout the day now. She just smiled and nodded. And the yellow tea they're bringing me, some barley and mint blend, it gives me the runs and I must speed over to the toilet every hour. Is there a seltzer bottle around here that someone could use to spray my face and crotch with, please? I'd say we're all set to remove the casts and send me back to my post now. How about it? I'm bellhop number six, not some invalid.

The doctor—I think the same one I last spoke with, but I'm not totally sure, they all have similar bushy black sideburns and bulbous noses—now tells me there's been an unexpected decline in my condition. I told him I'm feeling fine and better, though; all ready to go back to helping the guests with their luggage.

"My strength has returned, doctor."

"No, no," he clucked, "it seems to have spread to your spine."

"*What* has spread to my spine?"

"The fracture. This is certainly an odd case. Upon impact, as you know, your legs broke. Then there was a queer period of delay, perhaps your hindquarters put a temporary halt to the journey of the fracture, but now your spine is breaking up. Don't you feel it?"

"No, I most certainly do not feel it. What gives you this wild idea?"

"We noticed a quality to your posture as you slept in your chair, it is marked by a subtle but surefire undulation, and this gave us cause for alarm and we injected you with a strong anesthesia to conduct an in-depth five-hour examination. We x-rayed your spine. Here."

He pulled some sheets out from his lab jacket to show me.

"Look at all of those breakage points, the perturbing vascular appearance, if you will; veritable clusters of spinal rivulets. The disintegration isn't going to let up. We've got to solidify your spine with a network of rods and wires and screws, or else you're sure to permanently buckle up, and soon. In other words, yours is an emergency case, young man."

"How about an orange then?" It was the doctor, standing over me as I lay on an examination table.

"An orange? Why?"

"It will calm you down."

I'd never heard that one before, but I put my hand out and he gave me a freshly peeled naval orange.

"We're going to fix you up nicely, and you'll be back to work very soon," the doctor said as I chewed on the delicious juicy flesh. "The chief bellhop wanted me to tell you that you were doing a fine job and he eagerly anticipates your return to service. Now, turn over, we're going make an injection into your left buttock. This will put you to sleep, and then we shall wheel you into the next room and get started with the operation."

I was just starting to wonder if my grandfather had died amidst the fires when I felt the prick in my behind and quickly fell into a deep slumber.

During the operation I had a very slow dream of being stuck in a downtown Los Angeles elevator with a bunch of strangers. The sliding gate had a gold plaque screwed into it that said *Welcome to the Los Angeles Theater.* Initially, the riders didn't seem distressed by the halt of the elevator between floors, and a group of them continued their conversation about Denny Layer, the manager of my dreamland Dodgers.

"I saw him at Shawn's Grill in Brentwood last night, sitting alone in a corner booth. He was eating that towering meat lasagna and drinking orange juice after orange juice. Then first base coach Harry Hawkes stumbled in all drunk and disheveled wearing his cap backwards. Layer fired him right there on the spot, creating quite a stir. Several sportswriters ran over to the table and took the whole sequence of events down in their pads. We're sure to get the whole story in the afternoon papers."

"Well good riddance," replied one of the riders in a refined British accent. "Hawkes was always making such ridiculous mistakes, always calling after the runners that they missed tagging the base and must run on back, when the great majority of the time that most certainly was *not* the case. Often I considered him, actually, to be employed by an opposing team, perhaps the Giants—a saboteur, as it were."

Then silence fell, the ceiling light went off and the blades of the miniature corner fan stopped spinning. Everyone groaned. A moment later somebody passed a nervous and choppy flurry of gas. Usually in these situations I am overcome with panic. I hate being stuck, and before long I get to thinking that I'm going to die on the spot. Not this time, though.

I slid open the gate, and then slid open a horizontal porthole on the elevator door—the kind you always see in the movies depicting America during prohibition—and while all I saw in the elevator shaft were some meaningless serial numbers stenciled in glowing white paint on the black walls, I felt reassured and certain we would start moving any minute now, and that there was really nothing to worry about.

"Calm down everyone, we should be moving shortly. Just a routine drill—the building management is required to shut off the power unannounced at random times on a roughly quarterly basis to keep the population on its toes. Let's just relax and in five minutes you'll all be sitting at your desks, and then I bet some of you will wish you were still stuck in this here elevator. Am I right or am I right?"

My announcement eased the tension in the air of the cab. I suggested we all sing "99 Bottles of Beer on the Wall," which we did, and at nine bottles of beer the cables hiccupped, the light came back on, the fan spun once again, we continued our upward course—come to think of it I suppose I was the elevator boy—and I woke up.

"Have a postoperative orange, young man," said one of the doctors. "These babies just came in from the Mulholland Citrus Company, they couldn't have been picked more than two hours ago. Now please excuse the pun, but *you're back*."

"I'm *back*?"

"Yes, you're back—your spine is good as new. You might feel a little soreness and sensitivity over the next few weeks, so you won't be lifting and carrying any luggage around in the immediate future. But come tomorrow you should be back on your feet. Ross management has informed me that once you're feeling up to it you'll be assigned to the poolside newsstand and work there until you're ready to resume bellhopping."

In the pool area, the loudspeakers play a constant stream of jazz guitar music, and the sounds put me in a queer state of nervous calm. I'm wired, and also dull. I can't close my eyes, and it's difficult to stop staring at a given object once I've laid my eyes on it (some bright tabloid magazine cover, the cobalt blue flag on a pole affixed to the top of the lifeguard chair, the tall pink and white plastic wedding cake *Marry at the Ross* advertisement, etc.). The effect may be enhanced by the pills I'm now taking, a sedative that—according to the chief Ross pharmacist—"puts particular focus on the spinal-brain dynamic to dull the majority of post-operative pain and also will set your mind at ease following the potentially traumatic experience that is spinal surgery."

Sometimes I wonder if they actually even operated on me. Maybe they just put me to sleep and conducted an experiment. Maybe the experiment is still taking place. Gladly, the train of thought stops there, no sinister backgrounds come to the fore, and the sonorous interweaving lines of a game show trombone and a muted electric guitar shift my attention back to the hypnotic shimmering surface of the turquoise pool water.

"Hey, sonny, go bring a copy of today's *Mirror* over to

Jack at umbrella 20." Bruce, the head of the newsstand, occasionally rouses me from my stupors with some such instruction. I take a copy of the *Santa Monica Mirror* from the four-foot-high pile and walk it over to Jack.

"That's me on the guitar on this here song," he says. "'Fleur D'Ennui'—no one does it better than me. Just recorded this one last week at the Pacific Jazz studios in fact."

"Yes, Mr. Jack, it's very good. I like it." That's all I can muster for the dazed sunbather. He keeps a canvas bag full of pill bottles at the foot of his lounge chair and knocks back one caplet or another every half hour. More often than not, as opposed to reading, he makes whimsical pirate and baker's hats with the newspaper.

After making a delivery I'm fairly enervated and usually walk over to the bar and order a club soda and lime. I'm off sugar now—the doctors said it could interfere with my recovery.

At night, after I take my final pill for the day, I spend some time writing letters. They're quite short these days:

Joshua,
I'm here. Saw a limousine run over a pigeon this morn-
ing. Alright,
   Gregg

Dan,
Where do you get a bagel out here? We should open a
bagel place. What say you?
   Steve

Freddy,
I could write a list of grievances, but will save it for an-
other day. For now, all I have to report is that, in case
you don't know, in St. Vincent's Court there's a back en-
trance to the police station, special jewelry crimes divi-
sion.
   Sammy

I store them in the crate under my bed, the one that
used to house my cans of food. They feed me at the pool
now—mostly rye bread, margarine, pickles, and grape-
fruit—so there's no need to keep my room stocked. I've
lost a great deal of weight and have completely shed my
paunch. It doesn't look like I'll be returning to my bell-

hop position anytime soon. I'm too slow and weak for the heavy lifting. Fine with me.

My hours at the newsstand are settled now: I report to duty at half past seven in the morning and am stationed there until half past seven in the evening. I tend to fall asleep around nine o'clock with the jazz guitar echoing through my head, and sleep dreamless for ten hours straight.

Bruce said he would take me downtown to Clifton's Brookdale cafeteria for my 25th birthday next week. "They got a 20-foot indoors waterfall and live organ music and great turkey legs and jelly sauce. You'll have a fine time, sonny boy."

He asked me what kind of cake I like. I asked if they serve pie, and if so, how about a pecan pie? But the thought of that sweet brown gelatinous filling made me feel ill, and I spent the remainder of the afternoon hiding in the pool-staff WC.

I'm resting off the malaise in my room now, flipping through a few weeks' worth of newspapers I've saved up, and tearing out some images of New York; most of the Los Angeles papers include at least one photo of the damage in every edition, like the *Venice Evening Post-Gazette*, which maintains the rather sensationally named "MAN-HATTAN NIGHTMARE SCRAPBOOK."

I see that some of Lower Manhattan has gone up in flames too. "Let us mourn our fallen journalist brethren," one of the captions reads. "Here lies the *Sun*'s corner clock. It once proudly graced their Broadway headquarters, and now sleeps on the pave in a forlorn bed of sticks, pans, cooked pigeon corpses, and other indeterminate detritus. Alas, now the sun shines for none."

I've tacked this image on the wall next to my bed.

I asked Bruce for a cigarette this morning. I hadn't had one since a few days before I broke my legs. I went behind the newsstand to smoke it, and leaning against the shed I heard Bruce handling some horse bets. I never noticed him doing that before. I guess he's got a side-gig going. I don't feel like going to the cafeteria for my birthday tomorrow whatsoever, and I told him so.

"Whatever you say, sonny. If you want to take it easy the day you turn quartermaster that's up to you."

I almost asked him to stop calling me sonny but decided against it.

My birthday started out just like any other day at the pool. I brought the morning and afternoon papers to Jack, whose face gets redder by the day and who has developed quite the hacking cough, and otherwise just stood around nibbling on rye bread and drinking club soda and lime.

A major surprise around 4 o'clock in the afternoon, though: I saw my brother, wearing a panama hat and a pair of silver linen pants held up high by white suspenders, sitting at a table in the poolside bar area, having a meeting. I loitered behind him for a moment and heard him discussing flower ideas for the Ross lobby—"I'm thinking yellow orchids at the front desk and blue delphiniums at the coffee tables"—so I inferred that he's been hired as a consultant here.

I got up the nerve to tap him on the shoulder. "Good lord! I thought you were dead dear brother," he exclaimed, springing up and embracing me. "You're skin and bones here, what's that all about?"

I told him about my fall, the operation, the pills, and my current employment at the newsstand.

"We've got to get you out of here. This is no place for a young man—don't you see," he whispered. "Everyone here's all cracked up, damn it!" He turned back to his meeting. "Excuse me, Stanley, this here is my younger brother, whom I haven't seen in some time. I'd like to get him a nice lunch. Let me call you tomorrow and we'll finish our discussion over the phone, yes?"

He led me to the gurgling four-tier fountain beside the bar. "I'm going to have to sneak you out of here, I'm afraid. This is an asylum, for chrissakes, don't you know? How the hell did you end up here? No wonder you haven't reached me, the phones here are all dummies. Here, put on my hat, and tip it down over your face, and tuck your pants into your socks and let's hurry. I know a way out of the back that will take us right onto the crowded board-walk where we'll blend in."

He kept his hand on my back as we seemed to glide through a garden gate, down a few steps covered in fallen dry palm leaves, and then we landed in a thick crowd of amusement-seekers, children with faces covered in cotton candy and chocolate syrup, middle-aged men stumbling around in coffee-stained undershirts, and rosy-cheeked pairs of women strolling arm-in-arm.

"My car is parked in Venice, in back of the Cadillac Hotel where I had my first appointment today. Just a ten-minute walk through the throng."

"I can make it fine," I said.

We sped through a network of streets narrow and wide, passing every brand of gas station imaginable, making right turns and left turns and passing through back alleys and vast supermarket parking lots, and just when I had completely lost any sense of what direction we were traveling in, my brother announced, "A nice ride through Coldwater Canyon and we'll be at my place in no time. You remember my letters. It's one-story tall, in the shape of a cube, with a very high ceiling. A happy departure from whatever compartment the Ross surely had you holed up in."

"I'm looking forward to finally seeing the place. You know you're right, now that I'm thinking about it, something was a bit off about the place; my room was formerly a private sauna, and I suppose I may have been pushed around in a very silent way."

"More than off, I should say," my brother coughed. "The Ross is something of a nuthouse, and run by a bunch of crackpots."

His dismissal of the place as such confused me, and I didn't know what to think.

"How the hell did you end up there, anyway?"

After I told him he screamed in laughter at his reflection in the rearview mirror: "You walked right inside, of your own volition, thinking it a luxury hotel, and a swell place to work? Well, you know the line—Ah! How cheerfully we consign ourselves to perdition."

We parked on the sidewalk outside of his house—indeed, a tall white cube, and with several thin vertical windows running down all sides at uneven intervals. On his home turf, his manner of speech was more at ease, marked by a whimsical flourish.

"Welcome to Encino. It gets hotter here in the valley than what you're probably used to. Humid and dense, the deepest air California has to offer—good for the blood. Come in and let's get you some coco-nut water."

He opened his screen door with a tiny silver key that flashed in the sunlight and as we entered the house a sweet tropical breeze blew through all of the vertical windows producing a hushed sound like an exhausted church organ, and I felt a chill. I don't think I've ever witnessed —nor felt on my skin—such serene beauty. In the rear left-hand corner of the house is a thick patch of plants: cacti, jade, and aloe, finished off by a wall of beach grass that shoots along to the next corner and then curls around a ways along the right-hand wall.

"No flowers here," he said. "Flowers are for work. I like only green plants for the home. Up there, though," he pointed at a loft in the upper right-hand corner, accessible by an aluminum swimming pool ladder, "that's my office, where I keep my library of flower-related books."

Besides the plants on the floor and a table and chair and sagging bookshelf on the loft, the place is sparsely furnished, with two single beds (one situated along the right wall, under the loft and touching the end of the beach grass trail), and one along the left wall, next to a red Eames plastic rocking chair. Both beds are covered in thin Navajo-rug-patterned sheets. The only lamp is a big globular paper and bamboo one that dangles from the ceiling, and far underneath it stands a circular white table and three black wooden stools that look like flat-headed chess bishops. He picked up one of five coconuts from the center of the table, chopped off the top, and poured the fruit's water into a tall clear beer stein.

"I have a great health food store that carries these, fresh from Hawaii. Drink, and then rest. I've got a few hours of work to do, boring stuff—accounting mostly. We'll go out for dinner tonight. I must say that I became quite worried about you, and to my surprise really. You know, I thought I didn't give a shit about you anymore, what with your antics, poor instincts, and laziness. But you're my brother, and you're here in Los Angeles, and, all said, I'm glad. So rest up and then we'll go someplace nice and celebrate your birthday."

We went to an Italian restaurant on Victory Boulevard, a main drag in Encino. I hoped to find the towering lasagna from my dream on the menu, but found no such item.

I asked my brother, "Is there any restaurant in Los Angeles with a towering lasagna?"

"Not that I know of. Sounds unlikely. Why do you ask?"

"Well, I had a dream about such a place, and it doesn't seem so farfetched to me that it might actually exist out here."

"Sorry, just a dream. But the normal height lasagna here is very good."

I ordered it, and my brother had the shrimp scampi. I was feeling quite tired from the change in location, and wasn't really in the mood to chat about anything. He asked me what I plan to do now. I told him I haven't the slightest idea.

I've been shuttling all around this town for some time now, and just when I thought I was right about settled into my life at the Ross, my brother comes along and removes me from the premises. Sure, his home is a lovely place, but the novel beauty of it had already worn off by the time I awoke from my nap, and I know it's not for me. If there's one thing I've learned out here it's that I am happiest by the sea.

I diverted the subject of conversation away from my plans and asked him all about his flower business, half-listening to the answers and half-reminiscing about my life by the pool sipping club soda amongst the towers of newspapers. Now that was a good life.

My brother is out conducting business today at a number of hotels in Burbank. It seems the consulting side of his operation has really picked up.

"My eye has a fine reputation, if I do say so myself. Someday I think NBC shall be a client. I'll start with the common bathrooms, and work my way to on-set floral décor. Just wait. Then I'll be making big money."

Some of the turns of phrase he uses at home seriously aggravate me—he strikes me as a wimp when he's not driving me around and insulting me. I am seeing a whole different side of him, and am sorely disappointed.

This is supreme isolation here in Encino, and I don't

think I can tolerate it. The cube house gives me the impression that I am sitting in some kind of astronaut's decompression chamber; only I don't need to be decompressed, so in the end it has a compressing effect. I feel like I'm on the edge of Queens with no way out.

I figured a walk would lift my spirits, so I headed out the door for a closer look at Victory Boulevard. I passed a series of empty high schools and homes for the aged, and I saw a thin rocket launch off the grounds of a ranch not too far off in the distance, and the evacuated quality of the area made me want to crouch behind a parked car with flat tires and cry.

I walked into the convenience shop at a Chevron station to ask the man behind the register a question, but when I placed my hands on the counter I realized I didn't actually have any question to ask. *There are no buses to Santa Monica from here, you know that*, a voice in my left nostril whispered, *so there's no use asking him anything about that.*

"Can I help you, boy?"

"Ah, yes. You have any cigars?"

"No cigars. Cigarettes."

"Ah, no thanks."

"You alright boy?"

"Oh I'm fine, very good. Thank you! What was that a moment ago—some kind of rocket launch?"

"Military testing fields over there. They got the latest technologies going up, God bless it."

I was about to ask him if he had any updates on the situation in Manhattan, but decided I didn't want to hear anything else come out of this man's mouth. So I said thank you and walked out onto the deserted strip and headed back to the cube where I wrote some letters on my brother's stationary in the loft office.

Thomas,
The old fable of the west is stirring in the doorways, just look.
   Your friend,
   Jim

   Jim,
There's a show business tone to everything you say. Stop it. I will not open your letters anymore. Find a new correspondent-cum-therapist. I'm much too busy to humor you any longer. I have bigger things to take care of.
   Thomas

Thomas,

"Correspondent-cum-therapist"—what kind of phraseology is that? It amuses me to think I am writing you a letter that you won't even open. I should enclose your elegy in this one. Goodness, I have the shakes. What's so special about you? I guess I'll never find out. Goodbye now—

Farewell,

Jim

My brother came through the door around 7 o'clock in the evening with a stupid toothy grin pasted on his flower-pedaling mug.

"Real success today out there today, real success."

Before he had the chance to continue I told him that I'd been thinking about it and that I'd like him to take me back to the Ross tomorrow morning so that I can get back to work at the newsstand.

"Just like you were thinking about going to live with Jerry—always thinking—thinking ridiculous thoughts that get you nowhere but two-faced, lightning-struck environments—well no more of it. And I'll give you a good reason why. I happened to meet a nice fellow between meetings at the Burbank Hilton bar who writes a number of the ads that air during the NBC variety shows. Now I know it's not the movies, but I told him about you, how you're at loose ends, and after a couple of Seven & Sevens he said he'd be happy to help a young man in need of a position. There's an opening for a junior writer in his department. You'd contribute language to all the spots they show between sketches—you know, automobile ads, cereal ads, coffee ads, canned fruit and soda pop—whatever they need. What do you say? Well don't even bother saying, because you're meeting with him tomorrow afternoon for an interview. Now turn that frown upside down kid, because there's no room for sulkers in this town. Your meeting is at 2 and I'm taking you for a new suit in the morning. I'll fix us a big platter of rice and refried beans for dinner—you need to gain at least ten pounds, what'd they feed you at the Hotel Ross, seeds?—and then we'll turn in early. You've got a big day tomorrow, whether you like it or not. Take my advice, and like it."

In the morning my brother took me to a men's shop on the great deflated Victory Boulevard, which I have now decided is actually part of Nevada. The shop, Denny's Styles for Men, mostly carries western style garb—bright plaid shirts with long collars and silver snap buttons, thick dark blue jeans, sheepskin-lined leather vests, and Stetson hats—but they do have a small traditional formal wear section in the back. A gray mustachioed, short, plump, bald-headed man named Orlando assisted us.

"What can I do for you, what kind of suit today for the kind gentlemen, one for the both of you handsome lookalikes? We have the finest fabrics of Albuquerque just trucked in from yesterday. Fresh fabrics, they really stink of success."

My brother took the helm. "We're just shopping for the young man today. My brother, and he's got a big interview this afternoon with NBC and we've got to dress him up a winner. Nothing flashy, we need something classic, mature, and just a tad deferential. Navy blue."

"Well, why the young man appears so sour? Chirp up my friend!"

They proceeded to talk about me in the third person throughout the ordeal, and I forced a few smiles and took the last of my sedative pills in the dressing room as I slipped on a navy blue suit with gray buttons on the jacket, a white dress shirt, a red tie with little navy blue asterisks sewn in, and a pair of brown loafers. I presented myself and Orlando and my brother spoke simultaneously—

"Perfect."

"Orlando, fine work, he looks just right. We'll walk out wearing it. Let's go," he said, glancing at his watch. "It's already noon. We'll stop at a coffee shop on the way and have some fruit salad and cottage cheese for lunch."

My brother dropped me off in front of the Burbank Hilton and he told me to head straight through the lobby to the outdoor café, where I would find the man from NBC.

"Meet me back here at 3:30," he said, "I've got a quick meeting with the Van Nuys Airport management. Hoping to decorate their departure lounge. Good luck, Jacob."

I had imagined the interview would take place somewhere inside the NBC studios. Why we should meet at a hotel I couldn't understand, and it made me a bit suspicious. After all, my brother had already put me in a somewhat suspicious state of mind, what with his appraisal of the Ross, which didn't fully correspond with my own perceptions. I mean, it was certainly a *strange* place, but also a thoroughly *relaxing* place, and I just assumed that the doctors there subscribed to the West Coast school of medicine, hitherto unfamiliar to me. Anyway, it was in this conflicted mood that, upon seeing a tall orange haired man wearing a baseball cap emblazoned with the NBC peacock logo standing and waving his arms at me like a basketball coach, I didn't feel so sure that I should trust my interviewer. Maybe he's some kind of Palm Springs grifter, I said to myself, and I'd better watch out. He looks like a joke.

"So you must be Jacob, the famous brother. It's nice to meet you. Name's Jerry Cord. What a beautiful day, so clear. Would you just look at those San Gabriel Mountains?"

"Ah, Jerry. I had a friend named Jerry. In fact he's the reason I came out to Los Angeles. We were going to write scripts together. But that all kind of fell through."

"So that's what I hear. Sit down. Waiter! Get us a

pitcher of iced tea, extra lemon, sugar, and some mint sprigs if you have them, on the side.

"Well, I have a simple job to offer and I can see you're a smart fellow just by the skeptical expression on your face so I'd like to go right ahead and give you a shot at it; we'll just run with it and you'll learn as you go. Sounds good? Right."

I just kept nodding my head, tilted slightly to the right, up and down, and squinting my eyes.

"Are you familiar with Fresh-Up Freddie, the animated rooster mascot for 7-Up? OK, well that's a Disney creation, and at NBC we're in the middle of developing a bullfrog spin-off to promote Lay's potato chips—a hyperactive bullfrog, you see, who pours chips in bowls at all the hip parties, something like that, you get the idea—and a junior writer is needed to assist with the writing of these bullfrog scenarios. You're our man. Heck, maybe you can even come up with his name! Now how's all that sound to you, Jacob? Pretty good, I bet."

"Well, I certainly do appreciate the offer, and this sure sounds like a project I'd be proud to contribute to. Though if you'll excuse me I really must use the facilities, as I ate lunch very quickly and must have had nine glasses of water, and then I hope you'll allow me to ask you a few follow-up questions about the job. Sorry to jump up like this, but I'm sure you understand that when nature calls what can we do but take heed? Am I right? I'll be back in five minutes. Pardon me."

"But of course, go right ahead—the men's room is to the right of the lobby bar. I'll just be admiring those clouds rolling about the San Gabriel range, and don't mind if I do. Ha! I love it."

"Thank you, Jerry."

I shuffled off and loosened my asterisk-ridden tie.

After I used the toilet, the bathroom attendant squirted some soap into my palm. "Mouthwash?" he asked. I looked into his eyes—it was Jerry Stamp, and with a shaved head. So we were reunited again.

"Jerry? Is that you? I didn't recognize you at first, without hair."

"Jacob? You—I didn't recognize you. You've lost

weight. And that security officer's suit! What the hell are you doing in Burbank?"

"I'm meeting with some lout from NBC about a job. My brother set it up. What are *you* doing in Burbank?"

"Working. After I lost the script and you disappeared, and then that cat you took in jumped out of the window and got run over by an ice cream truck, well, I decided it was time for me to move on. So I found a job here, right where you see me, in the Burbank Hilton bathroom. I'm the afternoon attendant. Some cologne, *signore?*"

"Well damn Jerry, I ended up working in a hotel too, at the Hotel Ross in Santa Monica. I started as a bellhop, but then I broke my legs, and it got pretty complicated, and once I was back on my feet they transferred me to the poolside newsstand."

He handed me a paper towel, and I had an idea. "Hey! Come on Jerry, let's get out of here, Burbank is a bona fide wasteland. This whole area of town—it's not right for guys like us. Let's go west, to Santa Monica. I bet I can land us both easy jobs at the Ross. They'll surely let me back in, and we can start fresh, writing scripts at night. All kinds of people in the business take time out at the Ross, and everyone's so at ease that they'll be glad to have a look at our work while they loaf by the pool."

Jerry dropped the bottle of cologne on the floor. "Amen. That's what I like to hear. Let's get in my car—to the Hotel Ross, my friend, and the new life that awaits us."

We're safe at the Ross now. Jerry works in the men's bathroom-lounge by the pool, throwing talc at necks, spraying bare chests with cologne, spreading a fresh coat of pomade onto heads of hair, throwing towels over shoulders, and whatever else the male guests desire—a peppermint lozenge, a tonic, a pipe cleaner; Jerry's fully stocked. And I'm back at the newsstand with Bruce, surrounded by a miniature cityscape of newspaper and magazine piles, making the occasional delivery, and mostly just standing around in my white linen pants and t-shirt, chewing cinnamon gum, sweeping the floor. I wear a Panama hat in tribute to my brother, who has been permanently banned from the Ross for removing an employee from the grounds. He should have known better than to violate such a rule.

ACKNOWLEDGMENTS

Thanks to Paul Vangelisti, editor of *OR* at the Otis College of Art and Design, for publishing an excerpt of an earlier version of *The Wilshire Sun*.

Thank you Mom, D, and Matt for your love and support. Thank you Joshua Rahtz for the walks around old Hollywood; Michael Signorelli for your encouragement along the way; Rob Crawford for the close read; and Jonathan Rabinowitz for your care, sense of humor, and comfortable chair. Thank you Gabi Kozak for everything.